CW01348195

# Searching For Hope

## EMILY MARIE LOATS

WestBow Press
A DIVISION OF THOMAS NELSON
& ZONDERVAN

Copyright © 2020 Emily Marie Loats.

All rights reserved. No part of this book may be used or reproduced by any means, graphic, electronic, or mechanical, including photocopying, recording, taping or by any information storage retrieval system without the written permission of the author except in the case of brief quotations embodied in critical articles and reviews.

WestBow Press books may be ordered through booksellers or by contacting:

WestBow Press
A Division of Thomas Nelson & Zondervan
1663 Liberty Drive
Bloomington, IN 47403
www.westbowpress.com
844-714-3454

Because of the dynamic nature of the Internet, any web addresses or links contained in this book may have changed since publication and may no longer be valid. The views expressed in this work are solely those of the author and do not necessarily reflect the views of the publisher, and the publisher hereby disclaims any responsibility for them.

Any people depicted in stock imagery provided by Getty Images are models, and such images are being used for illustrative purposes only.
Certain stock imagery © Getty Images.

[Scripture quotations are] from the New Revised Standard Version Bible, copyright © 1989 the Division of Christian Education of the National Council of the Churches of Christ in the United States of America. Used by permission. All rights reserved.

ISBN: 978-1-6642-1081-3 (sc)
ISBN: 978-1-6642-1083-7 (hc)
ISBN: 978-1-6642-1082-0 (e)

Library of Congress Control Number: 2020921454

Print information available on the last page.

WestBow Press rev. date: 10/30/2020

# I

Nineteen years. I had nineteen years with my mom. I hope it was enough.

Now, I was going to have to take care of my little brother all on my own. I always knew that she was depressed. I had known that, since I was ten.

I had known it since my parents got divorced. All the signs of depression were there. The hopelessness, the panic attacks, the under eating, the over exercising, the low self-esteem. She was very sweet. She took good care of Daniel and me. She was just very depressed. Now, here I was Daniel's guardian at nineteen. I knew I wouldn't be able to tell him what happened. I was sure I knew what happened, when the police showed up. I made Daniel leave the room.

I still haven't told him what happened to her. I told him he's too young to know. I told him I'll tell him when he's older. He hasn't asked too many questions.

I've been too worried about making sure I get custody of him.

We've been too busy talking to social workers and going to court. Thank God, they let me get custody of him. They said they'll let me have custody of him because, I'm legally an adult, I have a job, and they want me and my little brother to, stay together. But, because, I'm so young, they said that they're going to have social workers come by and, checkup on us. They said if something goes wrong, he could be taken away from me. I was scared to death.

I didn't know how to explain what happened to Daniel.

"Rosie?", Daniel was giving me a concerned look.

"Yes?", I asked.

"Are we going to be okay?", Daniel asked.

I picked Daniel up, and I held him on my lap. I hugged him tightly. "We're going to be okay." I said softly.

I wasn't sure that I believed it, but, I needed to comfort him. Even though, he was ten, he was still my baby brother. "What happened to Mom?", Daniel sobbed. I held him even tighter.

"I can't tell you. You're too young to know. I'll tell you when you're older." I said. I was crying now, too. Daniel and I just hugged each other and cried. I couldn't tell him what happened to her. I just couldn't. He wasn't ready to know.

If he knew, it would make this even harder for him. He was too young to know. I'll tell him when he's older. I might wait until he's eighteen to tell him.

I just don't want to make it any harder for him.

After Daniel and I were finished crying, I put my arm around him, and I led him to my room. I've been sleeping with him, since Mom died. I've been holding him in bed every night. He has had a hard time falling asleep. Cuddling with him is the only way I can get him to sleep. I can't really blame him. Cuddling him makes me feel better too.

I remembered the first signs that Mom was depressed. Thankfully, Daniel was so young, that he can't remember most of it. Some of the worst of it, was right after the divorce. Daniel was a baby. She told me, that my dad left with another woman. I never saw him after he left. She told me that she was having panic attacks because she was so scared about getting divorced. She cried all the time. These were the first signs that she was depressed.

---

The next day, Daniel and I were eating pancakes for breakfast. "Rosie, when do you have to go back to work?" Daniel asked.

"Next, week. I'm going to bring you to work with me." I said. It's summer, so, Daniel is home from school. I work at a daycare, so, I'm going to be able to bring Daniel to work with me.

I really didn't want to leave him home alone. He's just a little boy. Daniel didn't say anything. He's been extra quiet since the funeral.

He really hasn't been himself. He was always funny, silly, playing, laughing, singing, and dancing. Since the funeral, it's just gotten worse. He's barely talking. He's crying all the time. He has trouble falling asleep.

---

"Daniel, come sit down with me." I said. Daniel and I sat down on the couch together.

"Daniel, you know that Mom loves you, right?" I asked. Daniel started crying.

"Yes.", Daniel said.

"Well, she still loves you now. She still loves you now, in heaven." I said.

Daniel started crying harder. I hugged him. Daniel and I hugged, while he cried.

"Daniel, would it make you feel better, if I prayed for Mom?", I asked softly.

"Yes.", Daniel sobbed.

"Okay. I'm going to pray. Dear, Jesus, please let our mom

be in heaven. Please, let her finally be happy. Please, let her finally be at peace. In Jesus's name, we pray,. Amen." I was crying now, too. Daniel and I hugged each other and cried.

"Do, you really think we'll be okay, Rosie?", Daniel asked.

"We'll be okay. When I take you to work with me, you can play with the other kids. You would like that, wouldn't you?", I was hoping that would make him feel better.

"Yeah. I'll get to play with the little kids?", Daniel asked.

"You'll get to play with the little kids." I said. Daniel is ten, so, he'll be one of the oldest kids there. I was hoping that playing with the kids would make him feel better. I had something to tell Daniel. Joy texted me and said she wants us to go to church with her again.

"Are you ready to start going to back to church with Joy?", I asked.

"Yeah. I like Joy. Remember when you and Joy used to babysit me together?", Daniel asked.

"I remember. It was fun. We'll start going to church with Joy again this week." I said.

# 2

It was glad that we finally had something to look forward to. Hopefully going to church would help cheer Daniel up. I knew he wouldn't be completely okay again for a long time. I knew that I wouldn't be completely okay again for a long time either. But, I really missed Daniel being his old happy, silly self. We were going to church at Calvary Chapel. We go to church with my best friend, Joy. I've been friends with her, since I was sixteen. I started going to church with her, a few months after, I started being friends with her.

I got baptized at the beach by her pastor. Soon, I started bringing Daniel to church with me.

Joy is my best friend, and she's a sweet girl. Her whole family goes to that church. They're all really religious Christians.

Joy was there, sitting with her parents. We sat next to her. Her older sister Grace was there, sitting with her husband, and her baby. Love. Her other older sister Ruth was there,

too. She was sitting with her husband, and her baby, too. Her older brother, Matthew, was there too. Joy is the youngest of her siblings. Matthew is the only one of her siblings who isn't married. Her sisters both got married and had kids, when they were young.

I wouldn't be surprised if Joy was married two years from now. We all listened to the pastor pray. He let us all give prayer requests and praise. He let all of us pray. Then we all sang upbeat worship music. Then the pastor read about how the fall of Jerusalem happened because, they left God. The pastor told us the reason we have so many problems in our country today, is because, we left God. Then, we sang more upbeat praise music.

"Hi, Rosie." Joy said. Joy was smiling, like always. The name Joy is perfect for her. She is sweet, happy, and beautiful.

"Hi." I said." I've been praying for you.

"I'm really sorry about what happened." Joy said.

"Thank you." I said. Joy hugged me.

"I've been praying for you. I'm going to keep praying for you.", Joy said.

"Thank you," I said. Joy looked over at Daniel. "I've been praying for you too, Daniel.", Joy said. Joy hugged Daniel. "Just remember that God loves you. I'll keep praying for both of you." "Joy said.

"Thank you. " Daniel said.

"You can always talk to me if you need to. And I'm going to keep praying for you." Joy said. I hugged Joy.

"Thank you. I love you." I said.

"I love you too." Joy said.

I almost always feel good with Joy. I almost feel good and happy after I'm done spending time with her. Even now, I feel better after spending time with Joy. She always shows me the love of Jesus. She's my best friend, and I love her. She's like a sister to me.

✧

"Hey, Daniel, do you want to draw with me?", I asked. Daniel really likes to draw. He's always really liked art ever since he was little. He loves to draw, color and paint. When he was two, he knew many famous paintings and famous painters. His favorite TV show when he was two, was about a little boy who loves art.

"Okay," "Daniel said, softly. Daniel still wasn't being himself.

I wanted to do something with him that he likes doing to make him feel better. Daniel and I sat down at the table and started drawing together. Daniel was drawing pictures of Phineas and Freb. I was drawing pictures of flowers and hearts. "You're a good artist, Daniel. You're doing a good job drawing.", I said.

"Thank you, "Daniel said. We sat and quietly drew pictures together for awhile. Daniel was being really quiet, just like he had been for the past few weeks.

I reached over and stroked his hair. "Daniel, I love you.", I said.

"I love you too. "Daniel said. "You can tell me anything. You can talk to me about anything. Okay?", I said.

I really wanted to help Daniel. "Okay." Daniel said.

I just stroked Daniel's hair, while he drew Perry the Platypus. Daniel didn't say anything else. He must not be ready to talk about it, yet. I'm just glad that he knows, when he is ready to talk about it, he can talk to me. I was laying in bed that night, and I was remembering how I saw all of the signs that Mom was, depressed.

I remembered how she told me she was having panic attacks because, she was so upset about, the divorce. I remembered her saying that my dad left with another woman.

I knew she was depressed because, of the divorce. She started being depressed after the divorce.

She told me how much the divorce upset her. She told me how much my dad upset her.

I knew how much my dad upset her. I knew how much the divorce upset her.

◈

I knew the divorce was why she was depressed. I knew my dad was the reason she was depressed. I ended up having panic attacks. I ended up having an anxiety disorder and OCD.

My mom told me I got it from her.

My mom told me she has depression and anxiety. I realized what low self esteem issues she had as I got older. She never ate enough. She exercised too much. She got plastic surgery.

She always worried that she wasn't beautiful enough. She doesn't need it. She is beautiful.

She's already beautiful, just the way she is. She's the most woman I ever knew.

She's perfect, just the way she is. She looked like a Barbie doll. She was that beautiful.

She had long blonde hair, blue eyes, and tan skin. She was tall and skinny.

She had straight white teeth. She wore pretty clothes. She was the picture perfect beauty.

She looked like a model. I would never live up to her beauty. I do look my mom.

But, her beauty will always be better than mine. I have her blonde hair and blue eyes. I have her face. But, I'll never be as tall as her. I'll never be as skinny as her. I never tried to be as skinny as her.

Watching her try to be skinny and beautiful looked exhausting. So, I never tried. But, I was happy that I look like her. I was happy when people said that I like her.

But, I'll never be as beautiful as her.

✧

I was always so close to my mom. I always loved spending time with her. I knew she loves me. She always told me and Daniel that she loves us. She always hugged us. She was really sweet to us. She spent time with us. She talked to us. She did fun stuff with us. She cooked for us.

She bought us presents. She taught me how to cook and clean.

I really love her. I told her I love her. I hugged her and kissed her. I told her she's beautiful.

I told her how beautiful she is.

I told her she shouldn't worry about how she looks. I told her, she's already beautiful.

I still love her. I just wish she understood her beauty and her value.

I wish she didn't have such bad self esteem. I wish I knew how to explain it to Daniel.

"I'm taking you to you to work with me today, Daniel." I said. Daniel was still being really quiet. I was hoping he would do okay.

Hopefully, playing with the kids will get him back to being his silly, happy, self again.

"They have Trolls toys at the daycare. ", I said this to cheer him up. "Trolls?" Daniel asked. Daniel looked excited. Daniel really likes Trolls. I was hoping he would like that.

"They have Trolls toys you can play with." I said. I smiled at his excitement. I pet his hair.

I work at a small daycare. It's a rainbow painted building with a rainbow painted fence.

It's a house that was turned into a daycare. There's about twenty kids in the whole building. There's a class for babies, a class for toddlers, and a class for older kids. I'm working in the class for older kids. Its called the Fairy and Elf Daycare.

Daniel will be one of the oldest kids there. Most of the kids are younger. I was hoping that Daniel would enjoy playing with the kids, and it would help cheer him up. I made the kids fruit loops for breakfast. Then they started playing. Daniel was playing with a little boy named Sam.

I was glad he was happy. Maybe, this would help cheer him up.

The kids were playing with toy animals and blocks. The rest of the day went pretty well.

We had singing and dancing time.

I took the kids outside to play on the playground. The kids played with toys. I read them books. We watched Peter Pan. It was a pretty good day. Daniel seemed to be feeling a little bit better. "Did you like going to work with me?" I asked. "Yeah. I liked playing with Sam." Daniel said. "Good. You can be friends with him." I said. I was glad that Daniel was starting to go back to being his old, happy self again.

"I'm glad you made a new friend. " I said. "Sam is nice. And he likes playing farm with me." Daniel said, cheerfully.

"was nice. Sam is a nice boy. He'll be a good friend for you. " I said.

"Do you think Sam can come over one day?" Daniel asked.

"Maybe. I'll have to ask his parents. " I said. This was a good sign.

Daniel really was starting to go back to being his old, happy, self again. I was glad he was starting to be happy again.

<hr />

That night, Daniel woke up crying. I woke up when I heard him sobbing.

"Daniel, are you okay?" I asked. I held him close to me. "I miss Mom." he sobbed.

I felt tears welling up in my eyes. I was crying now, too. "I miss her, too." I sobbed.

Daniel and I held each other and cried. "I had a bad dream. "Daniel cried." What was it about?" I asked. "I dreamed about the funeral." Daniel sobbed. He was talking between sobs.

I just held him. "Its okay. I miss her too." I said, softly. "Its okay to miss her."

Daniel and I just held each other tightly and cried.

The funeral was awful. I was wearing a black dress. Daniel was wearing a little black suit.

There were red and white roses. Daniel and I were both crying hysterically.

We hugged each other the whole time. The pastor prayed for Mom to be in heaven.

I prayed silently that she was in heaven. The pastor read about heaven in the Bible.

Then, we put rose's on her casket. I held Daniel into my chest,during the burial.

I wouldn't let him look. I wouldn't let him watch the burial. It would scare him.

I had my eyes closed the whole time. I couldn't watch the burial. It was be too painful.

I just hugged Daniel and cried the whole time.

Daniel and I cried ourselves to sleep that night.

The next day I sat Daniel down, and I told him I wanted to talk to him.

"Daniel, you can tell me anything. You can talk to me about anything. Okay?" I said. "I know." Daniel said. "Daniel, you can tell me what your feeling." I assured him. " I really miss her." Daniel sobbed. "Its okay to miss her. I miss her, too. I think that we should pray for her, okay?" I said. Daniel nodded. I held Daniel's hands.

"Dear Jesus, please let our mom be in heaven. Please, take good care of her in heaven.

Please, let us know that she's in heaven.

And, please, let us be with her in heaven one day.

In Jesus's name we pray, amen. " I prayed. Daniel and I hugged. "Thank you, Rosie."

Daniel said. "Your welcome. I want to help you.

I want to make you feel better. Jesus said he'll give us eternal life.

"For God so, loved the world that he gave his one and only son, so that he shall not perish but, have eternal life. For God did not send his son into the world to condemn the world but, to save, the world through him. However believes in him, is not condemned."- John 3:16.

"Jesus says that he'll give us, eternal life. So, we can believe that we'll see Mom again in heaven. " I said. "You really think that there's a heaven?" Daniel asked.

"I do. There are people who died and came back to life.

They said that when they were dead, they saw heaven. " I reassured him.

"I want to see Mom again in heaven. " Daniel said.

"We will." I assured him.

I decided to text Joy that night, and ask her to pray for us, and for Mom.

I'm really not a great person. I have messed up, a lot. The truth is, Joy is too good for me.

I really don't deserve her. I'm amazed that she still wants to wants to be friends with me.

I used to feel uncomfortable around her sometimes. She made me think about how I'm not good enough. But, because, she's so sweet, most of time she makes me feel happy.

Joy texted me and said of course she would pray for me, like always. I can never get over her. She seems so perfect. She's way too good for me. I don't deserve her.

I don't realize how lucky I am to have her. Don't think about it. Just think about how happy she makes you. Think about how happy she makes you. "Rosie, what are we having for dinner?", Daniel asked. "Tuna salad sandwiches, biscuits, and chicken noodle soup. " I said.

"Scrumptious!" Daniel said, happily. I smiled. Daniel is so cute.

I was glad that Daniel was starting to be happy again, like he always used to be.

Maybe we would end up being okay. I was still in very deep pain and, so was Daniel.

But, we were comforting each other. Joy was comforting us. God would help us.

We would probably end up being okay.

It was the first time that felt real hope in weeks. I remembered how Daniel always loved to sing and dance. I remembered how I would listen to music and dance with him.

I remember when we would color, and paint and draw together.

I remember when we would watch Disney movies and PBS kids cartoons together.

I remembered when I would tickle Daniel and he would laugh.

Soon, that happy silly, old Daniel was going to be back. We were going to be okay. We still had hope.

# 3

"Joy is coming over this weekend. " I said. "Okay." Daniel said.

Daniel had a cute little smile on his face. Daniel really likes Joy.

He always has. Joy and I used to babysit him together.

Daniel has really liked Joy ever since then. "Are we going to watch a Disney movie with her?" Daniel asked. "Probably. Joy likes watching Disney movies. " I said.

I remembered when I had a falling out with Joy. I was scared if she knew who I really was, she wouldn't want to be friends with me. I stopped being friends with her, because I was scared what she would think of me, if she knew, who I really was.

Joy kept praying for me. She texted me and said she wanted to be friends with me again, and she said she was praying for me. I started being friends with her again after that.

She helped bring me to God in the first place, and she helped bring me back to God, after I left him. I was scared she wouldn't like me anymore but, she still liked me anyway.

I really don't deserve her. She's too good for me. She's nearly perfect. I can never get over it. She's just so sweet.

I don't know what I would do without her. "Joy is here." Daniel said. "Okay, let her in." I said.

Joy is always sweet, understanding, happy, and sensitive. I love her. She's like a sister to me. She's my best friend. I'm always excited to see her. Daniel is always excited to see her too. Daniel really likes her. Joy had brought me a necklace and a bracelet that she had made me.

Joy had also brought cards she had made for me and Daniel.

"Hi, Rosie, I brought you presents." Joy said.

"Thank you. " I said. "I brought you something too, Daniel." Joy said. "Thank you, Joy." Daniel said. "Your welcome." Joy said. Joy handed me the necklace, bracelet, and card that she made for me. Then, she handed Daniel the card she made for him. Joy is so sweet.

She wrote on both me and Daniel's cards, that she's praying for us.

She wrote that she's sorry about what happened. She wrote that God will help us.

She wrote Bible verses about heaven and about how God loves us.

"That's so sweet of you. Thank you Joy." I said. Joy and I

hugged. "Your welcome." Joy said. "Thank you" Daniel said. "Your welcome. I've been praying for you.

I'm going to keep on praying for you." Joy said. We watched Lilo and Stitch together.

Joy and I did are nails and makeup, while we watched the movie. Joy did my hair.

We painted pictures together. We ate Oreos and drank hot chocolate.

We had fun with Joy just like we always do. I was glad that Joy came over.

She was helping me and Daniel feel better.

We were starting to feel like there was hope that we would be happy again.

We were still in pain but, Joy was helping us feel better. I'm not as innocent as people think I am. In high school people always said that I'm pure. It made me feel bad because, I'm not pure. People always said that I'm innocent. I'm really not. I always felt guilty around Joy.

I always knew that I would never be as good as her. I knew I would never be a good Christian.

I felt so guilty.

But, thankfully, Joy likes me. She's still friends with me.

And Jesus will still forgive me, when I ask for forgiveness.

I was thinking about it, when I was laying in bed that night.

I remember when I was so emotional, that I didn't know what to do.

I remember when I was watching porn and reading erotica.

I remember when I would get so emotional that I would cry all the time.

I would cry over Daniel growing up. I would cry over kids cartoons.

I would cry over Disney movies. I would cry over all of the bad things going on in the world.

I was crying over Daniel growing up all the time.

But, at the same time, I was looking at porn and reading erotica.

A part of me never wanted to grow up. A part of me wanted to force myself to grow up.

I was so emotional that I didn't know what to do. I had an anxiety disorder and OCD.

I was having panic attacks. I would get so emotional and so worried that I throw things.

I eventually broke my phone because, I felt so bad about watching porn.

I was extremely emotional. I didn't what to do. That was when I had my falling out with Joy.

I told her I didn't want to be friends with her.

I told her if she knew who I really was, she wouldn't like me. She kept praying for me.

She told me she was praying for me and wanted to be friends with me. We made friends again.

She still wanted to be friends with me. She still liked me. She showed me the love of Jesus.

I always wanted to keep Daniel innocent. That's why I always cried about Daniel growing up. That's why I don't want Daniel to grow up. I want Daniel to stay innocent.

I don't want Daniel to lose his innocence.

I don't want Daniel to learn about all of the bad things in the world.

I want Daniel to stay innocent. That's why I won't tell him what happened to Mom.

That's why I'm glad that he's young enough that he can't remember how depressed she was, right after the divorce.

I decided to write a poem about how I want Daniel to stay innocent.

I was hoping it would make me feel better. I got up and started writing a poem. *Innocent little one. That's how I want you to stay. I never want Dawn to turn into day.*

*I want you to always stay this way. I want you to stay innocent and creative.*

*Yes, Santa Claus is real. Yes, fairies are real. There is a Easter bunny. Trees can be purple. Whatever you dream can be real. Nothing is impossible. You can dream and play all day.*

*There is no evil. There is only good.*

*You can do whatever makes you happy.*

*You can always be happy and have fun. I want you to always stay this innocent.*

*I want you to stay in the innocence of Eden. I never want Dawn to turn into day. This is how I want you to stay.* I did feel a little bit better after writing the poem.

I thought that Daniel would like it. I wanted to show it to Daniel. I found Daniel in his room.

He was drawing pictures of me and him together.

"Hey, Daniel, that's a good picture. You're a good artist.

That's sweet of you to draw pictures of us together." I said. "Thank you." Daniel said.

"Daniel, I wrote a poem for you." I said. "What's it about?" Daniel asked. "Its about you."

I said. "Really?" Daniel asked. " I wanted to write a poem for you.

I've been thinking about how much I love you. So, I wrote this poem for you.", I said.

"Thank you." Daniel said. "Your welcome. Do you want me read it to you?" I asked. "Okay." Daniel said.

"Innocent little one.

That's how I want you to stay. I never want Dawn to turn into day.

I want you to always stay this way. I want you to stay innocent and creative.

Yes, Santa Claus is real. Yes, fairies are real. There is a Easter bunny. Trees can be purple. Whatever you dream can be real.

Nothing is impossible.

You can dream and play all day. There is no evil. There is only good.

You can do whatever makes you happy. You can always be happy and have fun.

I want you to always stay this innocent. I want you to stay in the innocence of Eden.

I never want Dawn to turn into day.

This is how I want you to stay." I read, aloud. "That's really nice. Thank you." Daniel said. Daniel and I hugged. "Your welcome. I'm glad that you like it. I said. "I want to stay innocent." Daniel said. "Good. I'm glad." I said.

Maybe Daniel will stay innocent. I just have to hope that he will stay innocent.

So, now I have hope that maybe Daniel will stay innocent.

I'd been thinking a lot about everything that happened.

I didn't tell Daniel because, I didn't want to scare him but, I was feeling really anxious and I was feeling kind of depressed. I was having a lot of painful feelings.

I was thinking anxious thoughts. I was feeling really down.

I tried to be happy for Daniel but, it was hard. Daniel was finally starting to feel happy again.

He still cried sometimes.

But, he was able to draw and listen to music and watch

Disney movies, and enjoy himself again. He was able to play with the kids at the daycare. He was able to be happy again.

Daniel was still in pain. I knew that he was. He still cried sometimes.

Every once in awhile he still had a nightmare. I let him cry when he needed to.

I told he could talk to me if he needed to.

But, most of the time, he was able to be play and be happy. I was glad he was happy again.

So, I tried to hide that I was still in pain. When Daniel wasn't in my room, I would cry.

I would only cry in front of Daniel if he was crying.

I didn't want to scare Daniel so, I tried to only cry when I was alone in my room.

I never told Daniel how much pain I was in because, I didn't want him to be scared.

It got so bad that I started wetting the bed. I decided that I needed to talk to Joy.

I would have to talk to her alone. I couldn't let Daniel hear what I was talking to her about.

I couldn't scare him. "Daniel, do you want to have a play date with Sam this weekend?" I asked.

"Yeah!" Daniel said, excitedly. "Okay, I'll call his mom and tell her."

I called Sam's mom and I set up a play date for Daniel.

Daniel was going to spend the weekend at Sam's house.

I invited Joy over to my house for the weekend. "Hi, Rosie. I've been praying for you." Joy said. "Thank you." I said. "Where's Daniel?" Joy asked. "He's at his friends house." I said.

"Oh. What's his friends name?" Joy asked.

"His name is Sam. He's made friends with him at the daycare." I said.

"Well, that's nice." Joy said.

"Yeah. I'm glad that he made a friend. He's been having fun playing with the kids at the daycare. Playing with the kids is making him feel better." I said.

"That's good. I'm glad he's been feeling better. So, Daniel's feeling better?" Joy asked.

"He's feeling a little bit better. He still cries sometimes. And he still has nightmares sometimes. But, he's starting to feel better. He's able to be happy and have fun." I said.

"That's good. I'm glad that Daniel is feeling better. So, how are you doing?" Joy asked.

"I'm trying to be happy for Daniel. Its really hard. Its still so painful.

I'm still thinking about everything that happened. I've been feeling really anxious.

I've been feeling kind of depressed." I said. "You can talk to me about it.

You can tell me anything.." Joy said.

"Thank you. I've been thinking about what happened a lot." I said.

"You can talk to me about it." Joy said.

"Well, I never really explained everything to you." I said.

"You can tell me about it. Its okay. You can tell me anything." Joy reassured me.

"She started being depressed after the divorce. My dad left my mom for another woman.

My mom told me how much the divorce upset her.

My mom told me how much my dad upset her.

I knew how much my dad hurt her.

My mom told me that she was having panic attacks because, she was so scared about getting, divorced." I said.

"Do you know why? Why was she so scared?" Joy asked.

"She told me that the divorce really upset her." I said. "That's terrible." Joy said." I know.

She was very depressed. She was sad all the time. She cried a lot.

She had depression and anxiety. She was sweet and she loves me. She was sweet to me.

I love her. I know that she loves me.

But, she was very depressed. These were the first signs that she was depressed.

Later, she started not eating enough. She exercised too much. She got plastic surgery.

She worried that she wasn't beautiful enough. She thought she had to hurt herself to be beautiful.

I guess, at some point her depression got worse. Later on, she started cutting herself.

I told her that I love her.

❖

I told that she's beautiful. I told her how beautiful she is. But, she was still depressed." I said.

"I'm sorry. Its terrible that happened. I've been praying for you.

I'm going to keep praying for you. "Joy said, softly. "Thank you." I said.

"You don't have to tell me but, I was wondering, how did she die?" Joy asked.

"She cut herself so much, that she bleed to death. She cut into her veins." I said, softly.

"I'm sorry. I'm going to keep praying for you. Just remember that God loves you.

Just remember that there is a heaven." Joy said "Thank you." I said.

"I love you. I'm going to keep praying for you." Joy said. "I love you too." I said.

Joy and I hugged. Joy and I spent the rest of the weekend praying.

We prayed that my mom is in heaven. We prayed that we will go to heaven.

We prayed for God to help me with my anxiety issues.

We prayed for God to help me and Daniel. We read the Bible.

We read what the Bible says about heaven.

We read what the Bible says about how much God loves us.

"This is my favorite Bible verse.

"Love is patient, love is kind, it does not envy, it does not boast, it does not dishonor others, it keeps no record of wrongs, it does not delight in evil, but, it rejoices with the truth.

Love does not easily anger. It always trusts, always hope's, always preserves. Love never fails.- 1Corinthians 3:13-16."

I said. "Why is that your favorite?" Joy asked. "Because, love is What's most important." I said.

"That's true. Love is what's most important. It says that in the Bible.

We were talking about that the other day at church. Jesus says that love is more important than the law. Jesus says that if your loving God and your loving other people, then your following the law." Joy said. "Love is what's most important." I said.

After my weekend of praying and reading the Bible with Joy, and talking to Joy, I felt better.

I was still in pain but, I was starting to feel better.

I was feeling more confident that there is a heaven.

I was feeling more confident that God will help me and Daniel.

Daniel and I were starting to feel better. We were getting comfortable with our routine.

Daniel liked playing with the kids at the daycare. He was happy being friends with Sam.

I was happy that I got to bring Daniel to work with me. I liked working at the daycare.

I love kids and working with kids makes me happy. Being around kids makes me happy.

I was still feeling really anxious. But, I was always able to talk to Joy when I needed to.

I was praying and reading the Bible. Spending time with Jesus helped me feel better.

Daniel and I were able to play together and have fun together again.

We were still in pain but, we were able to be happy again. Daniel and I were able to color, paint, and draw together. We were able to listen to music and dance and sing.

We were able to watch Disney movies and kids cartoons. We were able to cuddle. I was able to tickle Daniel and make him laugh. We were able to be happy and have fun again.

We were still in pain but, God was helping us heal.

# 4

I don't like to admit it but, sometimes, I think a lot how much I've messed up.

I start feeling really guilty. I start feeling distant from God because, I feel so guilty.

I start feeling depressed because, I feel so guilty. That's why I left God years ago.

Thankfully, Joy helped bring me back to God.

That night, I was thinking about how much I messed up.

I was thinking about it while I was laying in bed that night.

I had thinking a lot about how much I had messed up. I had been feeling really guilty because,

I had thinking about it so much.

I was remembering when I was watching porn. I was seventeen.

I had starting watching porn and reading erotica.

I felt really guilty about it. I felt so guilty about it that I broke my phone.

I knew that if I had my phone, I would feel tempted to do it, and I would end up doing it again. When I started doing it, it was just because, I was curious.

I didn't think that reading erotica was bad.

But, watching porn, I knew was bad. I felt really guilty about it.

I couldn't stop thinking about how those people were real people.

Those were real people, and they felt so terrible about themselves,

that they thought they had to have sex to make money.

They thought they couldn't do anything better. They thought they couldn't have a job where they didn't have to degrade themselves. They were giving up their freedom to make money.

They probably don't even want to have sex with those people.

Their probably doing it because, they feel so bad about themselves.

They gave up their self respect because they feel like they can't do anything better.

They might have been sex slaves for all I knew. They might have been forced into it.

And by watching it, I was supporting it. I was supporting degrading people.

I felt so bad about it, that I broke my phone. I wanted

to make sure I wouldn't watch porn again. That night, I was laying in bed and thinking about what I had done two years ago.

Even now, I still felt guilty about it. I'm a virgin but,

I know that I had committed a sexual sin by watching porn.

I knew that I had supported degrading people. I still felt guilty.

I knew that I wasn't pure. I knew that I needed to pray for forgiveness again.

I had prayed for forgiveness so many times but, I feel guilty anyway.

"Dear Jesus, please, forgive for my sins. Please, forgive me for watching porn.

Please forgive me for all of the sins that I have committed.

Please, help me to focus on you so, I won't sin. Please, let me go to heaven when I die.

In Jesus's name I pray, amen." I prayed. I felt a little better now.

I knew that Jesus would forgive me.

I laid down, and I went to sleep in remembered how the Bible says that Jesus wants to forgive, us. Jesus said he rejoices when we repent. Jesus said that he came to save us, not to condemn us. Jesus even forgave criminals, and prostitutes. Jesus came to forgive sinners.

Jesus wants to forgive me.

I realized that Jesus would forgive me, and I started to relax.

Daniel had started having nightmares again.

He had been waking up for the past few weeks crying.

He told me that he was having nightmares about the funeral.

I decided that to help him, I should have him read my favorite book, The Outsiders.

The Outsiders is by S.E. Hinton.

It's my favorite book in the world. I've read it 54 times now.

I read it for the first time in the eight grade.

My English teacher had us all read it in the eighth grade.

She's always been my favorite teacher ever because of that.

I love The Outsiders because it's such a beautiful story.

Its about loving people, and helping people, and believing that there's good in the world.

It shows that boys can and do express their emotions.

It shows that its okay for boy to express their emotions. It shows that boys can show love and affection.

It shows that siblings can have close and loving relationships.

Its beautiful and inspiring.

The Outsiders helped me a lot. It helped me believe that there's love and good in the world.

It helped me believe that boys can express their emotions.

It helped me believe that boys can show love and affection.

It helped me believe that siblings can have close and loving relationships.

Now, I'm going to have Daniel read The Outsiders.

I'm going to read The Outsiders with Daniel. I was going to wait until he was thirteen or fourteen to have him read The Outsiders but, now, with everything that happened,

he needs to read it now.

"Daniel, I have something for you." I said "What is it?" Daniel asked.

"I'm giving you my old book of The Outsiders." I said.

"Are you sure? Its your favorite book. You read it all the time." Daniel asked.

"I know. But, I have three books of The Outsiders. You can

have one of my old ones." I said. "Thank you, Rosie.", Daniel said. "Your welcome. I'm going to read it with you." I said.

"Okay. What is it about?" Daniel asked.

"Its about teenage boys with troubled lives. The main character is Ponyboy.

He's fourteen and his parents died in a car accident.

His older brother Darry got custody of him and his other brother Soda. Darry is only twenty.

He had to give up going to college so, he could get custody of his little brothers.

Darry had to get custody of them so, they could all stay together.

Darry has to have two jobs so, he can take care of them.

Ponyboy's second oldest brother Sodapop, dropped out of high school to get a job so,

he could help Darry with the bills. The Curtis brothers have very close and loving relationships with each other.

Ponyboy's best friend is Johnny and his parents abuse him.

Their group of friends show him the love and affection that his parents never did.

Ponyboy and his brothers, and their friends are greasers. Their the poor kids.

Their called greasers because, they have long, greasy, hair. The rich kids are the Socs.

Their called the Socs because, their socially elite.

The Socs bully the greasers, and they beat them up." I said.

"It sounds good." Daniel said.

"It's really good. It's a beautiful story.

It's the best book in the world. You have to read it." I said.

"Do you want me to read it because, the Curtis brothers are kind of like us?" Daniel asked. "That's part of the reason why." I said.

"Can we start reading it now?" Daniel asked. "Sure." I said.

We read the first two chapters of The Outsiders together.

Daniel really liked it. I could tell that he was really enjoying reading it.

I thought that he would be able to relate to it, and I could tell that he did.

"Who's your favorite character?" I asked, after we had finished reading. "Ponyboy or Soda." Daniel said. "My favorite is Ponyboy., I said. " I think that I'm like Ponyboy." Daniel said. "You are like Ponyboy." I said. "Can we read more tomorrow?" Daniel asked.

"Yeah. I would like that." I said. "I can tell why you like it so much now." Daniel said.

"Good. I'm glad that you like it. I though that you would like it." I said.

"I do like it. Its really good." Daniel said. "I'm happy that you like it." I said.

For the next week, Daniel and I read The Outsiders together every day.

Daniel told me how much he liked it. He told me how much he could relate to Ponyboy.

He told me that he's like Ponyboy. He told me that I'm a mix between Darry and Soda

. He told me that I'm a hard worker and a protective older sibling, like Darry

. But, he said that I'm sensitive like, Soda. I told Daniel, with how much were reading, we will be done reading the book by next week. By the end of the week we had read up to chapter six.

I really enjoyed going to church. I wanted to have a stronger faith and trust in Jesus. I wanted to start going to the women's Bible study at church. But, I would have to have Daniel sit by himself with the men and the children at Wednesday church, while the women's Bible study was going on in a different room. I wasn't sure if Daniel would be ready for that. I called Joy to ask for help. "Joy, I want to start coming to the women's Bible study with you., I said.

"That's really good. I'm happy that you want to come the women's Bible study with me."

Joy said. "Can your brother sit with Daniel while I'm going to women's Bible study?

I don't think that Daniel is ready to sit by himself at church yet." I said.

"Sure. I'll tell him to start sitting with Daniel at church." Joy said. "Thank you." I said.

I started going to the women's Bible study at church with Joy. I brought Daniel with me.

Daniel sat with Joy's brother in regular church while, I was in the women's Bible study.

I really liked going to the women's Bible study. It was fun and it was interesting.

It was me, Joy, and a few of the other women at the church.

Our group teacher taught us about the women of the Bible. She taught us about marriage.

She taught us about staying pure. She taught us about child birth.

She taught us about breast feeding.

She taught us about infertility. She was a foster parent so, she taught us about foster parenting.

She took things from the Bible, and she used it to teach us things that relate to women.

She took things from the Bible, and used it to teach us about infertility. She was really nice.

I really like her. I look up to her. I want to be like her. Our Bible teacher's name is Miss Rachel. I really like her a lot. I really like talking to her. She's a good woman.

She showed us that God really does care about women.

She showed us how to help children. The women's Bible study helped me grow closer to God.

After a few weeks of the women's Bible study, I was starting to feel better.

I was feeling less anxiety.

I was feeling a stronger relationship with God. I was having a stronger faith in God.

Daniel had been feeling better.

Between our daily prayers, our daily Bible study, our church twice a week,

and our reading The Outsiders, he was feeling better.

And having a friend and playing with the kids at the daycare helped too.

But, I could tell he was still in pain.

He got really quiet sometimes. Sometimes, he got really quiet, and his whole body tensed up.

I could tell just by looking at him, that he was in really deep thought.

One day, he was in really deep thought, and I decided to ask him what he was thinking about. "Daniel, are you okay?" I asked. "Yeah. "Daniel said. "Are you sure?" I asked.

"I can tell that you've been thinking a lot, lately." I said. Daniel didn't say anything.

"Daniel, you can tell me anything. Tell me what your thinking about." I said.

"I've been thinking about Mom." Daniel sobbed. "Daniel, its okay. Its okay to miss her.

I miss her, too. You can tell me anything. You can always talk to me about what you're feeling." I said.

I hugged Daniel tightly. Daniel and I hugged each other as he cried.

After a few minutes, Daniel was finished crying.

<hr />

"Do you want to pray? Will that make you feel better?" I asked. "Yeah." Daniel said.

"Dear, Jesus, please, let Mom be in heaven.

Please, let her know that we love her and we still think about her.

Please let Mom be happy in heaven. Please, take good care of her.

Please, let us be with her in heaven, one day. In Jesus's name I pray, amen." I prayed.

Daniel and I hugged each other. We sat quietly, hugging for awhile.

"Rosie, why did Mom and Dad get divorced?" Daniel asked, suddenly.

I really didn't want to answer that. Mom and I had always tried to shelter Daniel.

We wanted to keep him innocent. We thought because, he was young enough that he couldn't remember the divorce, it would be better if he didn't know about it. "Don't worry about it. I'll tell you when you're older." I said. "Are you going to get married, Rosie?" Daniel asked.

"I don't know. I'm know that I'm not going to get married anytime soon." I said.

"Do you want to get married?" Daniel asked. "Maybe. I don't know." I said.

"Will I get married?" Daniel asked. "I don't know, Daniel. You'll have to decide about that for yourself.

You'll know when you're older." I said. We didn't say anything else after that.

We just quietly cuddled.

# 5

The truth is that, I didn't know if I wanted to get married.

I had always been worried that marriage was scary. I had always been afraid of marriage.

I was worried that I wouldn't be able to know if I was supposed to get married.

I was afraid I wouldn't be able to know who I was supposed to marry.

I was afraid I wouldn't be able to know, if I would be able to stay married.

◈

I was mentally married to Ponyboy, though. I know it sounds silly but, its true. I love Ponyboy. If I ever get married, I want to marry a man who's just like Ponyboy.

Ponyboy is kind, sweet, innocent, caring, loving, sensitive, and affectionate. I love Ponyboy. Ponyboy is what's given me hope that there are sweet, sensitive, innocent, and affectionate men. It might sound silly but, its true.

And to me, its extremely important.

I never told anyone this but, The Outsiders is the only reason that I believe that men can express their emotions, and be sweet, and sensitive, and affectionate, and innocent.

The Outsiders is the only reason I believe that men can be good.

The Outsiders is the only reason I believe that I could ever love a man.

The truth is, I have a dark secret that I've never told anyone. I never even told Joy this.

I would never want Joy to know this. I would be too scared to tell her.

I'm afraid she wouldn't like me anymore.

I'm afraid her parents wouldn't let me be friends with her anymore.

When I was thirteen, I started thinking that I was a lesbian.

I thought I would never be able to love a man. I thought I would never be able to understand a man. I thought a man would never understand me. I thought a man would never love me.

I thought that men couldn't be affectionate, or sweet, or understanding, or kind, or loving, or, innocent.

I thought that only women could understand me. I thought I could only understand women.

I thought that I liked a girl I was friends with.

I started thinking about her a lot. I started telling her that she's pretty and beautiful, all the time.

I started staring at her all the time.

I hugged her all the time. Sometimes, we danced together.

When I danced with her, I would lean into her and lay on her. I played my had on her shoulder.

I even kissed her on the cheek a couple of times when I was dancing with her.

Then, one day, I told her that I like her. She never spoke to me again.

She told me she didn't want to be friends with me. She stopped talking to me.

I couldn't stop thinking about her. I thought about her all the time.

I read about being a lesbian online, just to be sure that I was. One day, I couldn't stop thinking about her. I wanted to prove to myself that I was a lesbian. I wanted to know I was for sure.

I didn't want to have to go through losing her for nothing. I wanted to get what I wanted.

I tried to kiss her on the lips at school.

She had the school switch all of her classes.

She didn't even want to be in the same class as me. I felt so guilty.

I felt so bad after I did it. I didn't want people to make fun of her.

I told the teachers that I don't want anyone to make fun of her.

They told me they'll make sure that no one makes fun of her.

Then, when I was fourteen, I read The Outsiders. My English teacher had us all read The Outsiders. I am so grateful. The Outsiders is the only reason I believe that men can be caring, loving, kind, sweet, sensitive, innocent, and affectionate. The Outsiders is the only reason I believe men can be good. The Outsiders is the only reason I believe that I could love a man.

The Outsiders is extremely important to me. I don't know if I'll get married or not.

But, I'll always be mentally married to Ponyboy.

If I ever get married, I'll only marry a man if he's like Ponyboy.

I'm extremely grateful that I read The Outsiders.

Maybe, God made sure that I was in the eighth grade English class where we all had to read

The Outsiders.

Maybe, God knew that reading The Outsiders was what I needed. I have messed up a lot. I have sinned. I'm not pure. But, I know that Jesus forgives me. Jesus said that he came to save the sinners. Jesus said, he rejoices when sinners repent.

Jesus happily forgives us when we ask for forgiveness.

I know that Jesus forgives me for my sins.

Jesus said that the one who has sinned little loves little.

The ones who has sinned much loves much. Jesus forgives me, even though I've messed up a lot.

✦

I wanted to talk to Joy. I wanted to ask Joy if she thinks I'll get married. Joy told me all about her older sister Grace, getting married. She told me that God told them that Grace was supposed to get married to her husband, Joseph. Joy told me that her mom read a Bible verse, and then she knew that Grace and Joseph were, supposed to get married.

Joy told me that she had to chaperone Grace and Joseph on their dates.

Because, their parents are so religious, they weren't allowed to be alone together until they were, married.

They weren't allowed to kiss until they were married. I know that Joy knows about marriage. Joy knows everything about her older sister's marriage. Grace's husband sounds really sweet.

Joy told me that Joseph went to their dad, and told him that he loves Grace and he wants to marry her. He said that he wants to protect her, and he wants to protect her purity. He said that he wouldn't hug her, or kiss her, or hold her hand, until their married because, he wants to protect her purity.

Joy knows about marriage. She watched her older sister's whole courtship with her husband.

Joy must know how to find a good man if, she saw her sister find a man like that.

I could never believe that she found a man who's so sweet and innocent.

If ever find a man like that, I'm going to marry him. I decided to talk to Joy about it at church that Wednesday, after church was over. I sat down with Joy, at one of the tables at the church. "Joy, I want to talk to you." I said. "Okay. What do you want to talk to me about?" Joy asked.

"So, do you think that I'm going to get married?" I asked. "I don't know. If God wants you to get married, he'll let you know that you're supposed to get married. If you are going to get married, you should marry a Christian so, that way you can have a Christian marriage." Joy said. "I wonder if I'm supposed to get married. " I said. "I don't know. If you're supposed to get married then, God will let you know that your supposed to get married.

God will speak to you and he'll let you know that you're supposed to get married.

I don't know how he'll speak to you but, he'll speak to you.

God will let you know that you're supposed to get married." Joy said. "Thank you." I said.

"Remember, the point of marriage, is to help you understand God's love for you,

and God's relationship with you. That's why it's so important to have a Christian marriage.

But, even if you don't get married, you're still the bride of Christ.

You'll always be married to Jesus." Joy said.

"Thank you, Joy. Your right. I need to remember that I'm the bride of Christ.

I need to stop worrying if I'm going to get married. It doesn't matter if I get married.

I'll always be married to Jesus. " I said.

※

"Your welcome. I'm glad that I could help you. Maybe you will get married.

A Christian marriage can be a great thing.

A Christian marriage is supposed to help you understand Jesus's love for you." Joy said.

"I'm not sure if I'll get married. If I do get married, I only want to get married if I'll have a Christian marriage." I said. "Maybe you'll get married one day. I'll be nice if you have a Christian marriage. "Joy said. "I don't know. I'll just have to wait and see." I said. Joy is right. Even if I didn't get married it doesn't matter. I'll always be married to Jesus.

I am the bride of Christ. I am Jesus's bride. I am Jesus's princess. Jesus is enthralled by my beauty. Jesus loves me. Jesus is my husband. I need to remember that. Even if I don't get married, I'll always be married to Jesus.

I had been thinking about Mom a lot lately. I really missed her. I was in a lot of pain because, I missed her so much. I was thinking about going through her stuff. I wanted to feel close to her again. I was scared to go through her stuff.

I was worried that it was going to make me miss her more.

I was worried that it would be too painful. But, I couldn't stop thinking about her. I just wanted to feel close to her again.

I couldn't go through her stuff in front of Daniel. It would make him miss her too much.

I decided that I would go through her stuff when Daniel was sleeping.

I went into the closet after, Daniel fell asleep. I was careful to be quiet so, I wouldn't wake Daniel up. I got out a box, that Mom kept all of her favorite memories in.

She called it her special box. I opened it up. There were some of my old baby clothes in it.

There were some of Daniel's baby clothes in it.

There were some my drawings that I made for Mom when I was little. There were some cards that I made for Mom. There were some letters that I wrote to Mom. There were some poems that I wrote for Mom. There were some drawings that Daniel made.

There some cards that Daniel made for Mom. There pictures of me and Daniel.

There were pictures of me and Daniel and Mom together.

At the bottom of the box, I saw something I never saw before. It was a diary.

✧

I opened it up.

It was Mom's diary. I didn't know that Mom had a diary. I started reading it.

I always knew that Mom was depressed.

It really helped me understand her thoughts and feelings.

She wrote about how she didn't think that she was pretty. I never understood why. I always thought that she was beautiful. She wrote about how she felt she couldn't trust people because, our dad cheated on her.

She wrote about how depressed she was because, our dad left her for another woman. She wrote about how she thought she couldn't trust people. She wrote about how she didn't trust men.

She wrote about how she had trust issues.

She wrote about how much our dad hurt her, and upset her.

She wrote about how lonely she was. She wrote about her depression and anxiety. It really made me understand how depressed she was. I started crying. It was so painful to read about how deep her depression and anxiety were.

I put everything back in the box. I put the box back in the closet. I got into bed, and I held Daniel. I cried myself to sleep.

# 6

It was so painful to know how deep Mom's depression and anxiety were. I had been thinking about it a lot since, I read her diary. I needed to talk to Joy. I was in a lot of pain.

I needed to talk about it. Daniel was starting to notice something was wrong. Daniel was asking if I was okay. I could tell that he was worried about me. I called Joy. "Hey, Joy." I said.

"Hi, Rosie. How are you?" Joy asked. "I need to talk to you. I've been feeling really upset." I said. "Why?." Joy asked. "I went through a box of my mom's stuff the other day. I found a diary she wrote in. I didn't even know that she had a diary. I read it.

She wrote a lot about her depression and her emotional problems." I started crying. "Its so painful to know how bad her depression was.

It hurts so much. I miss her so much.

It's so hard to know how bad her emotional pain was." I sobbed out. "You could pray about it. Praying about it would make you feel better. Do you want me to pray with you?" Joy asked. "Yes. Thank you, Joy." I said. "Dear God, please let Rosie's mother be in heaven.

Please, help Rosie believe that her mother is in heaven.

Please, let Rosie know that she will see her mother in heaven, one day.

In Jesus's name I pray, amen." Joy prayed. "Thank you." I said. "Your welcome, Rosie.

I want to help you." Joy said. "Thank you for helping me, Joy. I love you." I said.

"Your welcome. I love you, too."

Daniel and I were still reading The Outsiders together. We were close to finishing the book.

We were on chapter nine. Daniel really likes The Outsiders. I'm so happy.

I'm so proud that I had him read it.

I loved that me and Daniel were reading The Outsiders together.

"I can't believe that Johnny died from saving the little kids from burning to death. " Daniel said. "Don't worry. It gets better." I said.

"I really like The Outsiders. Its really good. I just cant believe that Johnny died from saving the little kids.

And then, Dallas died because, he couldn't live without

Johnny. He got the police to kill him on purpose." Daniel said. "I know. But, it gets better. I promise. You'll see." I said.

"I really like the part where Darry and Soda picked Ponyboy up from the hospital.

Its really nice how they all hugged each other.

And Darry cried because, he was so worried that Ponyboy died." Daniel said.

"I know. Its so sweet. That's one of my favorite parts. I love the Curtis brothers.

I love how much the Curtis brothers love each other. Its so sweet. I love The Outsiders.

Its my favorite book." I said. "I really like it too. I think The Outsiders is my favorite book now, too" Daniel said. "Good. I'm glad. I'm so proud." I said.

◈

Daniel was starting to feel better but, I knew that was still in pain.

I knew that he still missed Mom. He still cries sometimes. He's started having nightmares again.

I knew that I needed to do something to help him. Daniel woke up crying again.

He's been having nightmares all week.

His nightmares have been reoccurring off and on, ever since Mom died. They were going away for awhile. But, now, there coming back. I decided that I needed to talk to Daniel about it.

I knew that I needed to pray with him. I needed to talk to him about heaven. That's what would help him. "Daniel, you've been having nightmares every night this week. I need to talk to you about it.

I need to do something to help you.", I said, after breakfast that morning.

I had sat Daniel down on the couch so, I could talk to him. "I really miss Mom.", Daniel sobbed.

"I know. I miss her, too. Its okay to miss her. But, I don't want you to have nightmares.

I don't want you to be in so much pain. I want to help you." I said, softly. Daniel was crying.

"I want to pray for you." I said. I held Daniel's hands. "Dear Jesus, please, let Mom be in heaven. Please, let us know that Mom is in heaven.

Please, let us be with Mom in heaven, one day.

Please, help ease our pain.

Please, give us your strength, your love, and your peace.

Please, help us feel better.

Please, give us your peace.

Please, let Daniel stop having nightmares. Thank you for giving us your love. In Jesus's name I pray, amen. " I prayed. Daniel and I hugged. We were both crying. We just hugged each other and cried.

"Thank you, Rosie." Daniel sobbed. "Your welcome. I want to help you." I said. We just quietly cuddled. "Daniel, you know that there is a heaven don't you?

Jesus says that there are many rooms in heaven. He said that we will be with him, in paradise." I said. " I wonder what my room will be like." Daniel said.

"I don't know. But, I'm sure that it will be great." I said.

Daniel and I were still reading The Outsiders together. We were finishing the book.

We were on the last chapter now. I love the ending to The Outsiders. Its so beautiful.

It's the perfect ending. Its such a beautiful story. I love it. It's my favorite book in the world.

I can never get enough of it. "The ending is so good." Daniel said. "I told you that it gets better.

I love the ending. Its so beautiful. The ending is the best part. It's the perfect ending. Its so beautiful.", I said. "I really like Johnny's letter to Ponyboy." Daniel said. "I do, too. It's one my favorite parts.

And I really like Sodapop's speech to Darry and Ponyboy. Its so sweet. I love it when Soda tells them that they have to stick together because,

if they don't have each other, than they don't have anything.

It summarized the relationship between the Curtis brothers." I said. "I really like how Ponyboy said he wrote The Outsiders for his English class because,

he wants to help people believe that there's good in the world." Daniel said. "I love that part. That's one of my favorite parts. One of my favorite parts is Johnny's letter to Ponyboy.

I really like when he tells Ponyboy that there's still good in the world.

I really like when he says it was worth dying to save the little kids." I said. "That's my favorite part." Daniel said. "I love The Outsiders. Its such a beautiful story. It's the best book in the world. It's the most beautiful story in the world. I love it so much" I said.

"I understand why now. It's my favorite book now, too." Daniel said.

"I'm so happy. I'm so proud I had you read it." I said.

"Thank you for having me read it. I'm really happy you had me read it." Daniel said.

"Your welcome. I loved reading it with you. I'm really happy you like it so much. "I said.

I had been thinking a lot about heaven.

I decided that I needed to ask the pastor about it at church that week.

My pastor's name is Sam Willows. I really like him He's really nice. He's a really good pastor. I've talked to him before. He's really nice. I really like him. "Pastor Sam, I need to ask you something. "I said. "What is it?" He asked.

"What proof do you have that there's a heaven?" I asked. "I do have some proof.

I'm lucky that I have this.

This is something that I have, that most people don't have.

I have a friend who died, and she came back to life. She died when she was having dental surgery. She was gone for awhile. They brought her back to life. When they brought her back, she was crying. They thought that she was crying because, she was so scared. She said that, she wasn't crying because, she was scared.

She said she was crying because, heaven was so beautiful that she didn't want to come back.

She said that she saw her grandmother in heaven. She said that she saw her grandparents in heaven. She said that heaven was so beautiful, that she didn't want to come back. He said.

"That's amazing. "I said. "It is amazing. I'm lucky that I have that because, that's something that most people don't have. That was enough for me to believe in heaven.

It makes it easy for me to believe in heaven because, I have that.

There are other stories like that. There are other people who died and they came back to life again, and they saw heaven. So, I believe it. I do believe that heaven is real." Pastor Sam, said. "Thank you." I said.

"Your welcome. I hope that I helped you. "He said. "You did. Thank you." I said. "I'm glad that I helped you." Pastor Sam said.

That made me feel better. Hearing that story did help me believe in heaven.

Since I know that my pastor has a friend who died, and came back to life, and she saw heaven that made me feel better.

It made me feel better to know that she said that heaven was so,

beautiful that she didn't want to come back. Heaven must be real then. And it must be beautiful.

I decided that I needed to tell Daniel. It would make him feel better. When we got come from church, I decided I was going to tell him.

"Daniel, I have something to tell you. The pastor told me something that will make you feel better. " I said. "What is it?" Daniel asked. "I asked the pastor if he has proof of heaven. He told me that he does have some proof of heaven. He told me that he has a friend who died and she came back to life again. He told me that she saw heaven. He said that she told him that heaven was so beautiful that she didn't want to come back.

He said that when she came back to life, she was crying

because, heaven was so beautiful that she didn't want to come back.

He said that she saw her grandparents in heaven. " I said. "Really?" Daniel asked. "Really.

See, there is proof of heaven.

There is a heaven and its beautiful. heaven is going to be so beautiful,

that we won't want to come back." I said. "That sounds really nice." Daniel said. "It does. Does that make you feel better?" I asked. "It does." Daniel said. "Good. It makes me feel better, too." I said.

I wanted to feel closer to God. I decided to write in a prayer journal.

I wrote down all of my favorite Bible verses. I wrote about all the times in my life when I knew God had intervened.

I wrote down times in my mom's life that she had told me about when God had intervened.

I wrote down times in Daniel's life that my mom had told me about when God had intervened.

I wrote down times in Joy's life that she had told me about where God had intervened. I wrote down what my Mom told me about how, when Daniel was five and he was asking if, rainbows are real. She told me that she prayed for Daniel to see a rainbow because, she wants him to know that rainbows are real. The next day we all saw a rainbow. I remembered what my mom told me about her grandmother. She told me that she could feel her, grandmother's presence at her funeral. She told me that she could feel her grandmother hugging, her at her funeral. She said that she talked to other people about it, and they told her that they, felt the same thing. She told me that she knows that there is a heaven. I wrote down what my pastor told me about his friend going to heaven. I wrote down how I don't need to worry about marriage because, I'm married to Jesus. I wrote down that I'm not going to worry about marriage anymore because, I'm married to Jesus. I felt closer to God after writing in my prayer journal.

It made me feel better to write in my prayer journal. It helped me believe in God and heaven.

I was finally starting to feel a lot better. I was finally starting to feel a lot of my anxiety easing.

I was finally starting to feel more at peace. For the first

time in a long time, I really didn't feel that much stress and anxiety anymore.

I was still in a lot of pain.

But, now, I really was starting to believe that God had a plan for me, and he would help me.

# 7

I decided that was going to tell Joy that I'm feeling better, when I went to church that week.

I sat down with Joy, at one of the tables after church was over.

"What did you want to tell me?" Joy asked. "I've been feeling better.

I'm not feeling that much anxiety anymore. " I said. "Really? That's great!" Joy said. "I've been praying, reading the Bible, going to church, talking to the pastor, talking to you, writing in a prayer journal. I'm feeling a lot better, now." I said. "That's great! I'm so happy for you! I'm so glad that God is helping you." Joy said. "Thank you. " I said. "I've been praying for you. " Joy said. "Thank you. " I said.

"I was hoping that you would start feeling better. I'm going to keep praying for you. " Joy said. "Thank you. I love you. " I said. "I love you, too." I said. Joy and I hugged. I knew that Joy praying for me was helping me. Joy always makes me feel better.

Joy is the best friend in the world. She's so sweet. I really don't deserve her. I'm not saying that I still don't have problems. I do. I still feel anxious sometimes.

I'm still in a lot of pain. I still cry sometimes. Daniel still cries sometimes.

Daniel still has nightmares sometimes. I feel less anxiety now, though. I feel better now.

I feel more at peace. I feel hope. I know that God has plans for me. I know that God loves me and he helps me.

I know that God intervenes in my life. I know that God will help me and Daniel. I know that God will take care of us. I think it's hard for a lot of people to understand.

I remember in high school, people said that I'm pure. They said they can tell I'm a virgin.

They said they can't believe that I'm waiting till marriage. Some of them said they've already had sex. I'm waiting till marriage because, I know that I'm married to Jesus. I know that I'm the bride of Christ. I know that marriage is supposed to help us understand Jesus's love for us,

and his relationship with us. I know that if I have sex before marriage, it could cause trust issues in my marriage.

I know I could get an STD. I know I could get pregnant. It's not because, I don't think about sex. I do think about sex. I do want a boyfriend.

But, I know following God's plan is better.

I know God's plan is good. I know that God created is plan to be good for us.

It's not because, I'm pure. I'm not pure.

It made me feel bad when the kids at my school called me pure. I'm not pure. I've watched porn. I've read erotica. I've thought I was a lesbian. I've tried to kiss a girl. I think about sex.

I'm not pure.

I'm waiting for marriage though because, I know that God's plan his good. Its not that I don't have problems. I do. It's that I know God has plans for and he'll help me.

That's why I feel better.

And just because you want to wait until your married, doesn't mean you never think about sex.

I do think about sex. I just know that I'm going to wait until I'm married to have sex because,

I know that sex outside of marriage is dangerous. Just because, I messed up, that doesn't mean that God doesn't love me.

Jesus still loves me even though I messed up. Jesus forgives me of my sins. Jesus said that he came for the sinners. He said the sick need the doctors. He said that those who have been forgiven much, love much.

Jesus said he rejoices when we ask for forgiveness. Jesus wants to forgive us. Jesus is happy when we ask for forgiveness. Jesus forgives us of our sins. Jesus died so, he could forgive us. Jesus loves us even though we sin. Jesus forgave prostitutes and criminals.

Jesus promised a criminal on the cross that he would be, with him in paradise. Even though we aren't pure, Jesus loves us and he forgives us.

---

Daniel had been doing better for awhile. His nightmares weren't reoccurring. But, suddenly his nightmares were back. I was worried that his nightmares weren't gone. His nightmares have been reoccurring on and off, ever since Mom died. Daniel had woken up screaming and crying.

I was glad that he had been sleeping with me. I held him close to me. "Daniel, its okay. It's just a nightmare. Its just a dream. Its over now." I said, softly. "Rosie, I miss Mom." Daniel sobbed. "I know. I miss her too. Its okay to miss her.

She's in heaven. We'll see her in heaven, one day." I said. "What happened to her?

What happened to Mom?" Daniel sobbed. "I can't tell

you. Your too young to know. I'll tell you when you're older. We can pray for Mom tomorrow." I said. Daniel cried himself to sleep, while I held him. I wondered if maybe, I should tell him.

I wondered if maybe, he wouldn't be able to feel better until I tell him. Maybe, he needed the closure. Maybe, he couldn't really heal, until he knew what happened.

I started to wonder how I could tell him what happened. The next day, I sat Daniel down on my bed. I told him I wanted to talk to him. "Daniel, I want to pray with you. " I said. "Okay. " Daniel said. I held his hands.

"Dear Jesus, please, let Mom be in heaven. Please, let us know that Mom is in heaven.

Please, help us ease our pain. Please, give us your strength, your love, your faith, and your hope. Please, give your peace. Please, let us be with Mom in heaven one day.

In Jesus's name, I pray, amen." I prayed. "Thank you, Rosie." Daniel said. "Your welcome.

I want to help you.", I said. I was quite for a minute. "Daniel, I need to talk to you.", I said. "What's wrong?"

Daniel asked. "I think I should tell you what happened to Mom. I don't think you'll be able to heal, until you know what happened. I think that you need the closure." I said. "What happened?" Daniel asked.

"Mom was very depressed. Do you know what that means?" I asked. "No. " Daniel said.

"She was sad all the time. She was very overly emotional. She had a lot of very strong feelings. She wasn't able to control her emotions. She was so emotional that she didn't know what to do." I said. "But, why did she die?" Daniel asked.

"She was very depressed. She was very emotional. She was so emotional that she didn't know what to do. She didn't know how to control her emotions.

She had bad self confidence. She was insecure. She felt bad about herself.

She felt like she wasn't good enough." I said. "But, why did she die?" Daniel asked. "She cut herself. She cut herself so much that she bleed to death." I said. "Why did she cut herself?" Daniel asked. His innocence made this even harder. "She wanted to die. She made herself die." I said. "She made herself die?" Daniel asked. "Yes." I said. "Why did she want to die?" Daniel asked. He was so innocent. His innocence made it so hard to tell him. That's why I didn't want to tell him. "She killed herself." I said. "Why did she do that?" Daniel asked. "She was so emotional that she didn't know what to do. She was sad all the time. She felt bad about herself. She thought that she wasn't good enough. She was depressed. She had bad self esteem." I said. Daniel started crying. I hugged Daniel tightly. I was crying now, too. "She loves us Daniel.

She just thought that she wasn't good enough. She was so emotional that she didn't know what to do. But, she loves us. You know that she loves us.

Didn't you notice how she was sad a lot? Didn't you notice how she worried so much about, how she looked? That's because, she was depressed. She had bad self esteem.

But, she loves us Daniel. One day, we will see her again, in heaven." I said, softly. I hugged Daniel tightly. He was still crying. "Why did she feel so bad about herself?" Daniel asked.

"I don't completely understand. She thought she wasn't good enough. She got divorced.

I think that's part of the reason why she was depressed. She worried that she wasn't beautiful enough. That's part of the reason why too." I said. "Why did she want to die?" Daniel asked.

"I don't completely understand. She was worried that she wasn't good enough.

She was so emotional, she didn't know what to do. But, she loves us. I know that she does."

I said, softly. Daniel and I hugged each other and cried. We quietly cuddled. I hope that now Daniel knows what happened, he can heal.

I hope that now, he can find the closure that he needs. I hope that knowing what happened, won't make it worse. "I still don't understand why she felt so bad about herself." Daniel said.

"Its okay. I don't completely understand either. She was worried that she wasn't good enough. She was depressed. She was so emotional that she didn't know what to do.

She was sad all the time. I don't completely understand why. Part of it is because, she got divorced. Part of it is because, she worried that she wasn't beautiful enough. But, she does loves us Daniel. I know that she does. You don't have to worry about why she felt so bad about herself. She's in heaven now. One day, well see her again in heaven." I said. "Do you think she's happy now?" Daniel asked.

"Remember what the pastor told me? He said when his friend went to Heaven, it was so beautiful that she didn't want to come back. Everyone is happy in heaven." I said. "Well, I just hope that she's happy now." Daniel said. "She is." I said. "Daniel, do you know what Mom told me?" I asked. "What?" Daniel asked. "She told me that when her grandmother died, she could feel her presence at her funeral. She said that she could feel her grandmother hugging her at her funeral. She told me that she talked to other people about it and, they told her that they felt the same thing. She told me that, she knew that heaven is real. She's in heaven Daniel. I know that she is. And one day, we'll see, her again in heaven." I said. "That makes me feel better. Thank you Rosie." Daniel said. We just quietly cuddled for awhile.

# 8

I really didn't want to have to tell Daniel what happened to Mom.

But, I think that this is going to give him the closure that he needed.

I really don't think he can heal without knowing what happened to Mom. He still seems confused.

But, his nightmares have been reoccurring less often. Maybe, this is the closure that he needs.

I have been praying with Daniel a lot. I've been reading him a lot of Bible verses about heaven. I've been taking him to church a lot, too. He seems to be doing better. I'm glad that his nightmares have been reoccurring less often.

I don't think that they'll completely go away for a long time. He's still in pain. I knew that I needed to ask him how he's doing. "Hey, Daniel, are you okay?" I asked, one morning.

"I'm okay." Daniel said. "Are you sure?" I asked. "I don't know."

Daniel sobbed. He suddenly started crying. "Daniel, its okay. You can always talk to me" I said. I hugged Daniel while he cried.

"Daniel, can you tell me what your thinking about? You can tell me anything . You can tell me what your feeling and what you're thinking." I said, softly. "I really miss Mom. " Daniel sobbed. "Its okay. I miss her, too. Its okay to miss her.

You can always talk to me when you need to. She's in heaven now, Daniel.

You need to remember that. In heaven there's no pain. There's no tears. There's no sadness. There's singing. There's angels. There's light, and crystal clear water. There's fruit trees. There's golden streets. There's a pearl gate. Heaven is beautiful. Mom isn't in pain. She's happy now. One day, well be there with her. You need to remember that." I said. "Thank you, Rosie. That makes me feel better." Daniel said. "Your welcome. I want to help you." I said. "Even though Mom is happy in heaven, I still miss her." Daniel said. "That's okay. I miss her, too. Its okay to miss her." I said. I held Daniel's hands. "Let me pray with you." I said. "Okay." Daniel said. "Dear Jesus, please,

let Mom be in heaven. Please, let her know that we love her.

Please, let us know that Mom is in heaven. Please, let us be with her in heaven one day.

Please, let Daniel not have nightmares anymore. Please, ease our pain.

Please, give us your peace, your, love, and your hope. In Jesus's name I pray, amen." I prayed. "Thank you, Rosie." Daniel said. "Your welcome. I want to help you. Just remember that we'll see Mom again in heaven." I said. Daniel and I hugged. I decided that I was going to tell Joy that I finally told, Daniel the truth.

I saw Joy at church that Wednesday. I pulled her into a room that was empty. "What is it?" Joy asked. "I told Daniel what happened to Mom." I said. "What did he say? Was he upset?"

Joy asked. "He was upset. But, I tried to explain it to him. And I told him that she loves us.

I told him that we'll see her again in heaven." I said. "Why did you tell him?

You said that you didn't want to tell him. You said that you wouldn't tell him until he's older." Joy said. "I know. But, he was asking what happened. I think he needed to know so, he could have closure." I said. "Is he doing better now?" Joy asked. "He's doing a little bit better.

His nightmares are reoccurring less often. I'm helping him.

I'm reading him bible verses about, heaven. I'm praying with him. I'm telling him Mom is in heaven. I'm telling him that we'll see her again in heaven." I said. "Well, that's good. I'm glad that he's doing better. And hopefully, going to church will help." Joy said. "I think that going to church is helping." I said. "Well, that's good. I'm glad that going to church is helping. I'm still praying for you guys.

I'm going to keep praying for you. I'm glad that you talk to me.

You can always talk to me about anything. You can tell me anything." Joy said. "That you. I love you." I said. "Your welcome." Joy said. We hugged.

"Thank you for helping me." I said. "Your welcome. I want to help you." Joy said. We sang lots of songs at church. We sang Jesus Loves Me, This Little Light Of Mine, and Silent Night. It was beautiful. I put on Lauren Daigle music in the car, on the way home. We listen to You Say and Trust In You. I love Christian music. It's beautiful. I was finally starting to feel better.

I was finally starting to feel at peace.

For the first time in a long time, I felt at peace. Daniel was feeling better, too.

He was calmer, less anxious. He was happy again. He was playing, he was singing, dancing, coloring, drawing, and painting. He was listening to music. He was playing with me. He was playing with the friend Sam. He was playing with the kids at the daycare. He was watching Disney movies. He was watch kids cartoons. Daniel was finally starting to be his old, happy self again. Then, I looked out the window and saw a rainbow. I remember when my mom told us that she prayed for Daniel to see a rainbow, and the next day we all saw a rainbow. "Look, Daniel, there's a rainbow. " I said. "I really like rainbows. There so nice." Daniel said. "I really like rainbows, too. Rainbows are God's way of giving us hope. Rainbows give us hope of God. In the Bible, God told Noah, that he created the rainbow, to give people hope." I said.

Daniel was finally starting to be at peace. God was helping us. We could feel the love of God.

We felt at peace for the first time, in a long time. For the first time in a long time, we felt hope. We knew that God would help us. We knew that God would take care of us. We knew that God loves us. We knew that God is present in our lives. We knew that God would help us and give us his, peace, his strength, his love and his hope. We knew that when we were searching for hope, we just needed to look to Jesus, and he would help us. We knew that we didn't need to search for hope anymore because, we had found our hope in Jesus …

# Works Cited

*The Outsiders,* S.E. Hinton, Viking Publishing, Puffin Penguin Publishing, 1967.

You Say, Lauren Daigle. Trust In You, Lauren Daigle. Times New Roman Catholic Bible, Corinthians 3:16.

Times New Roman Catholic Bible, John 3:16.

# About the Author

I'm Emily Marie Loats. I'm nineteen years old. I wrote Searching For Hope because, I wanted to write a Christian book, that was realistic. I didn't want it to be about the perfect Christian girl, with the perfect Christian life. I wanted to show people that even though, you have problems, and you mess up, you can still be a Christian. I wanted to show people, that even though you don't have the perfect Christian life, and you don't have the perfect Christian family, you can still be a Christian. I also, wanted to talk about mental illness. I have Asperger's syndrome, OCD, and anxiety. Talking about mental illness is important to me. I wanted to talk about how, even though you have mental problems, you can still be a Christian. I wanted to show that God can give you hope. I knew girls in middle and high school who tried to kill themselves. I had a friend in high school who texted me one day, and she told me that she tried to kill herself. I knew a girl in high school, who missed school pretty much all of eighth grade and ninth grad because, she tried to kill herself. She ended up dropping out. I wasn't friends with her. I had classes with her. I wished I could help her but, I didn't know what to say. Now, I wish I could go back, and say something to help. I knew a girl in tenth grade, at church who tried to kill herself. Mental illness is important to me. I know what it's like. I have mental problems. I wanted to show that God can give you hope. I wanted to help people understand the pain of divorce. My parents got divorced. It did cause pain. I don't think people understand. I remember when I was younger, I talked about it, and people didn't understand. I wanted to make people realize, that whatever it is someone is struggling with, you shouldn't be judgmental. Jesus told us not to judge anyone. I wanted to help people by writing this book. I want to help people understand that God can give you hope. I remember in my senior year, I tried to talk to kids about God. I tried to help them. They would say, "Well, I'm doing this, and this so, I'm not going to be a Christian." I tried to help them. I tried to talk to them about God. They would say," I'm doing these things, so I'm not going to be a Christian. " They told me about all the things that they were doing. They told me about there family problems. And they said that won't be a Christian.

I wanted to write to this book to help people. I want to want to help people understand, that even though they mess up, and even though they have problems, and even though aren't the perfect Christian, with the perfect Christian life, and the perfect Christian family, they can still be a Christian. I wanted to help people understand that God will forgive you. I wanted to help people understand that God will give you hope. I wanted to help people understand that you shouldn't judge anyone . I wanted to help people understand that, instead of judging people you should try to help them, and understand them. I wanted to help people believe in God. Sincerely, Emily Loats